GRANDMOTHER AND HER SUITCASE

GRANDMOTHER AND HER SUITCASE

PART I — THE FUR COAT
On Mercy That Saves a Life

PART II — THE UNDERGROUND WORKSHOP
On the Price of Freedom

PART III — GRANDMOTHER AND HER SUITCASE
On a Home That Cannot Be Bought

by
Alex Avetis

Sometimes an entire life
fits into a single suitcase.

First edition

ISBN: 979-8-9949132-6-0
Published by Alex Avetis Publishing
Las Vegas, Nevada, USA

For information, contact: www.alexavetis.com
Printed in the United States of America

AUTHOR'S NOTE

Some stories are never told.
Not because they are unimportant,
but because they are too close.

They live inside families —
in the pauses between sentences,
in gestures passed down from one generation to the next,
in fears we cannot explain,
and in choices we make without fully understanding why.

Such stories rarely appear in books.
They contain no heroism in the usual sense,
no clear answers, no graceful endings.
Only life —
as it truly unfolds.

Boris's grandmother lived several lives.
She lost her home, her loved ones, her country, her language.
And each time, she began again —
only to lose everything once more.

Yet one thing remained:
the ability to keep moving forward,
even when there was nowhere left to go.

This is not a biography.
Nor is it an attempt to preserve the past "as it really was."
The past slips away regardless.

This book is an attempt to preserve what remains —
what a person carries within
when war, a system, or circumstance
takes everything else away.

Sometimes it is a fur coat.
Sometimes it is fear.
Sometimes it is love.
And sometimes it is a small suitcase
that somehow holds an entire life.

I did not write these stories to explain or justify the past.
I wrote them so as not to lose what matters most —

the memory of a choice
that makes a human being human.

— Alex Avetis

TABLE OF CONTENTS

PART I

"If a life can be reduced to an
object and a decision, then there is hope."

14

15

PART I

THE FUR COAT
On Mercy That Saves a Life

Grandmother and Her Suitcase

16

*Be a little more compassionate—
to others and to yourself.*

Never give up.

A miracle will find you.

Grandmother and Her Suitcase

This story is about Boris's mother and grandmother.
And about a fur coat.

An ordinary, heavy winter coat with a black collar —
a coat that came close to death more than once,
and each time chose life.

Because of this coat, they survived the war.

Kaunas. Before the war

Boris's mother was named Hana.
His grandmother was Feiga. In Hebrew, Feiga means "bird."
Perhaps that is why she spent her whole life on the move — like a
bird in search of freedom.

Hana was eleven years old. She was a happy child, unusually
mature for her age — with rosy cheeks and light, curly hair, lively
and carefree.

They lived in Kaunas, Lithuania, together with Hana's parents, her three-year-old brother, and her grandmother, in an apartment on the third floor.

Below their home was a grocery store owned by the family.

To reach the apartment, one had to walk down a long corridor. On the right, near the front door, there were coat hooks. Hanging on one of them was a heavy black winter fur coat with a fur collar.

At the end of the corridor was the kitchen, always filled with the smell of fresh bread. White lace curtains hung in the rooms. The house was always clean and calm.

In 1939, when the Red Army entered Lithuania, Hana's parents were allowed to sell everything in their store — but only for Lithuanian currency.

The Russian officers had only rubles. The parents accepted them, hoping the money would still be useful.

To keep it safe, Hana's mother sewed the banknotes into the lining of that same black fur coat with the fur collar.

That was 1939.

Now it was 1941.

June 22, 1941, was a warm day — almost festive.

No one yet knew that on this very day, the world they were used to would come to an end.

Without warning, Hitler's army invaded the Soviet Union.

By that time, Lithuania was already part of it.

Hitler had already persecuted thousands of Jews, although many had managed to flee to other European countries.

By evening, German troops were approaching Kaunas.

Little Hana and her family still did not know that this was the day their calm, happy life would end forever.

Panic spread through the city: some hurriedly closed their shops, some tried to sell off their remaining goods for next to nothing, others ran back and forth between home and the train station, unable to decide whether to flee or stay.

Hana's mother began quickly selling everything that was still left in the store. No one knew what tomorrow would bring.

A few hours later, a friend of Hana's father burst into the apartment. He was pale and spoke in fragments.

He had heard from a Russian major: the Germans were about to enter the city. They would do terrible things to the Jews. The only chance to survive was to leave immediately.

"The last train leaves in a couple of hours," he said. "After that, there will be no trains."

It was the last chance.

In a rush, dressed for summer — believing they were leaving for only a few nights — Hana and her family, along with hundreds of other Jews, ran to the train station.

Before leaving, Hana's mother took a few pieces of jewelry and their passports and put them into a small suitcase.

Running through the corridor, she took the black winter fur coat with the fur collar off its hook — so that her grandmother would be warm at night.

In the rush, thinking only of warmth, she completely forgot about the money sewn into the lining.

The bombing

The train consisted of open freight platforms — the kind normally used to transport livestock. But it was the only way to escape. People climbed on however they could. The train headed east — somewhere into Russia. That was all they knew.

Four or five hours later, German planes began bombing the train.

In Belarus, the convoy came under a massive air attack. Bombs fell directly onto the cars.

The German planes appeared suddenly.

They flew low and struck the train with precision.

Explosions tore through the train.
Cars caught fire.
People screamed.

Panic broke everything.

Some jumped from the platforms.
Others ran without direction.

Bodies already lay on the ground.

The air filled with voices —
people calling names, searching for one another
through smoke and fire.

A woman sitting next to Hana was hit.
Her blood splashed across the girl.

For a moment, her parents thought Hana herself was wounded.

Then they understood —
it was not her blood.

Many were killed.

In the chaos, families were separated; people shouted names,
searching for one another through smoke and bodies. Hana's
grandmother lost everyone for a time as well. The wounded lay
everywhere — groaning, crying, calling for those close to them.

By some miracle, they found each other again.

The train stopped in the middle of a forest. It was night. In the
darkness, the simple fact that they were together again already felt
like a miracle.

Some people went back to the shattered cars to search for their
belongings.

Hana's father refused — he did not want to rummage among the
dead.

All that time, Hana's mother never let go of the heavy fur coat.

The Barn

*A*ll the survivors walked in the direction the train had been heading before the bombing. It was getting cold. The mother draped the fur coat over the grandmother's shoulders.

Along the way, she noticed an elderly woman walking alone. She was shivering from the cold, wearing only a thin cotton dress. Without hesitation, the mother took the coat off the grandmother and placed it over the old woman's shoulders.

No one was thinking about money then.
They were thinking only about life.

The old woman walked ahead and soon disappeared from sight.

That night, a group of families with children found several barns standing in the middle of a field. People climbed inside, hoping to survive until morning.

Soon they heard the roar of motorcycle engines.

No one knew who it was — Germans or their own.

The men peered through the cracks.

They were Germans.

The cold inside the barn was deadly.

They could feel it in their bones.
In their hands.
In their breath.

Hana's little brother began to cry.

At first quietly.
Then louder.

The grandmother pressed him against her,
trying to warm him with her body.

It didn't help.

The child cried harder.

The sound spread through the darkness —
thin, sharp, impossible to ignore.

Someone whispered: "Make him be quiet..."

Another voice, lower, urgent: "Please..."

No one moved.

No one knew what to do.

Outside, the engines grew louder.

Motorcycles.

Closer.

The men crept toward the cracks in the wood
and looked out.

Germans.

The word passed silently, without sound.

Inside the barn, everything tightened.

The child was still crying.

The grandmother closed her eyes.
Held him tighter.

But the crying did not stop.

It only grew.

A few people turned their heads away.

Others stared into the dark.

Waiting. For what would happen next.

And then —
out of the darkness — a figure appeared.

The same elderly woman.

She stepped inside without a word.

In her hands — the coat.

She came closer.
Gently placed it into the mother's arms.

No explanation.
No hesitation.

The mother wrapped the child in it.
The crying stopped.

At once.

As if it had never been there.

The Germans rode past.

The sound moved away. Slowly.

Then disappeared.

No one spoke. No one moved.

Only the cold remained.

And the quiet.

If they had found the people, they would have burned the barn down
with everyone inside.

The coat returned to the grandmother's shoulders.

They were still alive.

The Last Train

The next day, at first light, they set out again. Staying in one place was dangerous — the Germans could return, and there was no food.

To avoid starving, people dug potatoes out of the fields, gathered berries. Some had suitcases with food and shared what little they had left.

They walked for two days, sleeping in the forest.

Hana's mother spread the heavy black winter coat with the fur collar on the ground so that the grandmother and the small child could lie on it and not freeze.

The coat became a bed.
Then a blanket.
Then the only protection against the cold.

On the third day, the group of families reached a small railway station in Belarus, not far from the Russian border.

There they heard that a train bound for Siberia would soon pass through.

Russian soldiers were at the station. They allowed the people to board the train — they knew the Jews were fleeing from the Germans.

Everyone boarded the last train heading east.

No one knew where it would take them.

Only that it was moving away from death.

The station stood on the edge of the front line.
People waited for that train
as for their final chance.

Such is a person's fate —
to catch the last train of salvation
more than once.

It felt as if they traveled for an entire week. From time to time, the train stopped at small stations, where kind people brought them water and a little food.

...At last, they arrived in Novosibirsk — the capital of Siberia.

Siberia

Novosibirsk greeted them with cold.

Russian officials distributed all the Jews among collective farms, where they were to work as hired laborers in the fields. By then, severe frosts had already set in.

Hana's family and a few others were given some clothing to cover themselves, but it was not enough.

People died from cold, hunger, and disease.

From July to November 1941, Hana's family lived and worked there.

Terrible cold and hunger ruled everywhere. People died right on the streets. It became clear: if they stayed, they would not survive until spring. They would not survive the cold or the hunger.

Hana's father was a calm man. He said little and did his work.

Her mother was anxious. She thought constantly about how to save the family.

One day she learned that Kazakhstan, far away from there, had a much warmer climate and that conditions for Jews were better.

And so she began to make a plan.

First, they needed to get their passports back — the Russian officials had confiscated them upon arrival in Novosibirsk.

She knew that without money, it was impossible.

And then she remembered the Russian rubles.

The money had been sewn into the lining of the heavy black winter coat with the fur lining.

She found the coat, ripped open the lining — there was enough money to pay the officials for the passports and to buy tickets to Kazakhstan.

Grandmother Feiga waited for the right moment to go negotiate.

She decided that at night, when everyone was asleep, she would try to speak with the officials.

But before that meeting could happen, the irreparable occurred.

Death

One morning, Hana's grandmother did not wake up.

In Siberia, cold and illness take quickly.
They do not forgive weakness.

She was buried beside the house where they had been living.

The family stood around the grave.

No strength for grief.

No strength for farewell.

Only breath turning into frost.

A prayer —
barely audible.

Then silence again.

After that, everything became clear.

They would not survive here.

Not the cold.
Not the hunger.

Not the winter.

It was a choice.

Life or death.

And she had already made it.

For them. Without asking.

At any cost.

Hana's grandmother was wrapped in that same fur coat and buried.

The one that had saved them on the road.
Warmed a child in the barn.
Gave them money to live.

It was the very coat that had saved their lives more than once and given them hope for the future.

Together with the grandmother, they buried the past they had lived through.

But the coat — as memory of the past and remembrance of her — remained with them forever, in their hearts.

Kazakhstan

After the burial, in the middle of the night, Feiga went to the Russian officials. They agreed to take the money in exchange for the passports.

Then she went to the chairman of the collective farm, laid everything that remained of the sewn-in money on the table, and said:

"These are all the funds we have. Please take us to a place from which we can leave for Kazakhstan."

"I will do everything," he replied, seeing the money.

The chairman took the money and promised to drive them to the station himself.

He gathered the family, put them on a cart, and took them to the station.

He placed the entire family on a train to Kazakhstan — to Taldy-Kurgan, to warmer lands.

The coat saved their lives once again.

Without it, they would have perished in that hell.

In Kazakhstan, the air was different.

Not warm — but survivable.

They met a woman who took them in.
Quiet. Kind.

There was still a little money left.
Enough for a room.
Enough for food.

Life did not become easy.

But it became possible.

And that was enough.

Later, the family moved into a small apartment and stayed there until the end of the war.

They lived poorly, with hardship — but they lived. They survived until the war ended.

When peace was declared, they were able to return to Lithuania.

Return

Many years later, Grandmother Feiga came to Siberia to find her mother's grave. She hoped to transport her remains back to Lithuania.

But the village no longer existed.

In its place, there was only an empty field.

Perhaps the people who once lived there did not survive that hell.

But they did...

Feiga thought that the coat that had saved their lives had remained there — together with the past that could not be brought back. Its spirit was somewhere there now as well — together with her mother.

And it became easier for her.

*The coat traveled a long road with them —
it saved an elderly woman on the road,
a child from the cold in a barn,
and an entire family from death in Siberia.*

This is a story about mercy that saves from inevitable destruction.

*When life is under threat and you lose those close to you, there is
nothing more valuable than life itself —
not money,
not possessions,
not wealth.*

*Sometimes, when we find ourselves in a hopeless situation,
we wait for a miracle.*

*We search for it somewhere far away.
We pray. We hope.*

But often, the miracle is already near.

*You only need to see it.
Or it will find you on its own.*

*Sometimes, a miracle is not salvation —
but the simple fact
that you are still able to wait.*

* * *

"Silence was not safety. It was survival."

Grandmother and Her Suitcase

PART II

THE UNDERGROUND WORKSHOP
On the Price of Freedom

42

43

Freedom isn't the absence of chains.

Freedom is the price you pay.

This is not a story about a crime, and not about heroism.
It is about how ordinary people learned to survive inside a system
where fear was the norm,
and gratitude was a way to stay alive.

The House

In Vilnius, in a private house, the whole family lived together: the grandparents, the parents, Boris, and his little sister. At the time, the sister was only one year old.

The house had a large cellar. All kinds of things were stored there — old belongings, tools, and supplies for the winter. The cellar was deep, dry, and convenient. And it was there that a story began — one the family would later avoid speaking about aloud for a long time.

Boris's grandmother was a strong, practical woman. She had golden hands: she cooked beautifully, knew how to sew, hem, and repair any clothing. In those years, under Soviet rule, there was a total shortage of everything. Obtaining good-quality items was almost impossible.

And one day, his grandmother had a bold idea.

The Underground Workshop

In the cellar, she set up a small underground workshop for sewing leather goods. A separate room was built below.

Inside stood two sewing machines, a lamp with a lampshade, and stacks of cut pieces of leather. Above, on the floor, lay a rug — for camouflage.

If you lifted the rug, a door leading down was revealed.

Private enterprise was harshly punished. It was considered a serious crime. For any "extra word," for any attempt to run a business — no matter what kind — one could receive a sentence for life.

Everyone knew this.

Uncle Lyova

A year before the events described, the family already had a terrifying example — the story of Uncle Lyova.

He worked as a truck driver in the fields. They grew potatoes in the village and transported them to the city. When tractors dug up the potatoes, they were loaded onto trucks, and Lyova drove the load to a warehouse, from where everything was later sent for sale.

One day his truck was loaded with potatoes. He had been working since morning and hadn't had time to eat. His home was along the road to the warehouse. He stopped by the house and went in to eat.

Someone informed the authorities that while on duty, with a load of potatoes, he had stopped at home and might have stolen part of the harvest.

The KGB came for him. He was arrested.

He received ten years in prison with confiscation of all property.

The grandmother knew all this.

But she still decided to go ahead.

Work

Two women worked for her in the underground workshop. They were paid well by the standards of the time. In the city, the grandmother sold nothing. All the goods went to the countryside, where people knew one another. People came to her to buy boots.

The boots were beautiful, made of genuine leather.

The grandfather worked at a leather factory. From there, he brought home scraps of leather — what was thrown into the trash bins.

Every day before work, the grandmother packed lunch for him in a small plastic container. After his shift, the grandfather would walk past the dumpster where leather waste was discarded and stuff the container with pieces of leather. Then he brought them home.

From these scraps, the grandmother sewed boots, slippers, handbags, and other items. Everything was made with design, with a sense of taste. The goods sold quickly. Orders increased.

The money was good.

And that was precisely what made it dangerous.

The Search

One of the neighbors informed the authorities that something suspicious was happening in that house.

One day, officers from OBKhSS burst into the house — the Department for Combating Theft of Socialist Property. They were feared more than anyone.

For the smallest act of private enterprise, they could hand down a life sentence.

They came with witnesses, with paperwork, with cold faces. One of them sat at the table and began inventorying all the property. The others spread through the house, conducting a search.

Boris was small. He sat in a corner and watched what was happening, not understanding anything.

In the wardrobe in the father's room lay a large amount of cash — earnings from the grandmother's sales.

If the money were found, it would mean prison and exile for the entire family.

When they tried to enter the father's room, the father sharply stopped them.

"Get out of my room. You came to search my mother-in-law — search her," he said firmly. "This is my room."

Boris's father was known in the city, so they treated him with caution.

"No," the senior officer replied calmly. "This is one house. We will search everything. We'll start with her room, then the entire house."

They overturned furniture, opened wardrobes, searched — without really knowing what they were looking for.

In the father's room, they found the money — a large stack of cash earned from selling the grandmother's goods.

The money lay on the table.

Counted.
Neatly stacked.
Exposed.

No one spoke.

The mother swayed —
then collapsed.

The father did not move.

"These are my personal funds," he said calmly.
"Please don't touch them. Conduct your search and look for what you need."

"You live in the same house," the senior officer answered calmly. "We are obliged to inventory and confiscate them. Later, if the money is legal, you may get it back."

When the counting was finished, the father placed his hand on the money and took it from the table.

"Put the money back on the table. Why are you putting it in your pocket?" the senior officer asked nervously.

"First, it's my money. Second, I will go with you myself and hand it in myself. And wherever I hand it in, that's where I'll retrieve it from."

He demonstratively put the money into his pocket.

At that moment, the little sister was in the room.

She began to cry.

The mother was on edge, rocking the baby, trying to keep her quiet.

But the child squirmed and screamed.

Meanwhile, the OBKhSS officers were searching another room. Everyone was ordered to sit still and not move.

"Don't you hear the child screaming?" the father said loudly to the mother, so everyone could hear.
"How many times have I shown you how to rock a child properly, so she doesn't cry?"

He took the child from her, began rocking her — and quietly transferred the money from his pocket into the baby's swaddling cloths.

The mother came to her senses.

She understood what he was doing and whispered in Yiddish:

"I know what you're doing. Don't be crazy! Give them the money! God help us — let them take it. They'll put us all in prison."

He did not answer.

When all the money had been hidden in the swaddling cloths, the father said:

"Put our daughter in the crib and sit beside her. Rock her until she falls asleep."

The mother went into the room with the child.

In the crib lay their daughter — wrapped in swaddling cloths stuffed with money.

The father stayed behind, waiting for it all to end.

The Reckoning

The senior officer looked around the house and suddenly asked:

"Tell me, please — this painting here, how much is it worth approximately? If you don't know, we have specialists who can determine the price."

"We think about a hundred rubles," they answered.

He walked over to the refrigerator, opened the door, and smirked.

"No specialists needed here. Judging by the food alone, you spend at least two hundred rubles a month."

He walked through the house, pointing with his hand:

"This rug here — no less than three hundred rubles."
"A Pobeda car in the garage — that also costs a fair amount."

In fact, there were two cars. One was in another garage and registered in the name of Boris's aunt.

They inventoried everything: furniture, kitchenware, tables, chairs. The senior officer named deliberately underestimated prices — as if doing them a favor.

"Now let's calculate your total income," he said.

"You," he addressed the mother, "are a teacher. You earn about seventy-five rubles."
"And you," he looked at the father, "work at the taxi depot. You earn around one hundred twenty."

He added the figures.

"So your household income is about two hundred rubles a month. Please explain where the money for all this property comes from."

There was nothing to answer. Everyone was silent.

The search ended. They did not find the underground workshop. No valuables either.

Only small pieces of leather were discovered under the bed.

The father was taken away.

The KGB

The mother burst into tears.

"What are you doing… You won't come back from there…"

The father, as always, remained calm. He hugged her and left with the officers.

The family spent the entire night in total uncertainty.

In the morning, the father returned home and told them what had happened next.

At the KGB building, he was taken into a separate room.

"Sit here. Put the money on the table. Someone will come shortly, count it, and formalize the confiscation."

"Wait a moment," the father said calmly. "Sit down."

"There's nothing to put on the table. I have no money."

"What do you mean — no money? We counted it! You took it!" the inspector protested.

"There is no money. You may search me."

The father stood up and raised his hands.

The inspector searched him and nervously asked:

"Where is the money?"

"That's where you're mistaken," the father said. "You think I believed I would ever get it back?"

"I decided it would be better to give that money to poor people who have nothing to eat."

"While we were driving, I opened the car door slightly and handed the money out to people on the street. Now go and collect it back."

The inspector turned pale.

"How am I supposed to prove now that the money even existed?"

"Let's do this," the father said. "So, your head stays on your shoulders, and mine too. Take the document where you listed the money and tear it up."

"I don't know — and you don't know. But at least ordinary people got something. Let's end it there."

The senior officer understood everything. He led the father out of the building through the back entrance.

That was how the father escaped certain prison — thanks to composure and intelligence.

The Price of Freedom

But the grandmother was imprisoned.

They found several pieces of leather under her bed. That was enough. The conclusion was immediate: if her husband worked at a factory, then he must have been stealing.

Why the grandfather was not arrested — because the complaint had been filed specifically against the grandmother.

When the grandmother was taken away, the grandfather lay down to sleep without undressing.

He was stunned and broken.

All the money they had earned was hidden in the toilet — on the pipe behind the toilet bowl. They had installed a second pipe and hid everything there: gold, diamonds, jewelry, money.

The grandfather took money from there and gave it to people, trying to save his wife. People came and said they had "connections" to a judge.

Some simply took the money and disappeared.

Others were more "cultured" swindlers: they took the money, promised help, then returned part of it — just in case she might be released.

When the pipe was empty and the money almost gone, the grandfather finally found a real approach to the judge.

But in doing so, he exposed himself.

Someone informed the KGB that the grandfather had a lot of money and was spending it to secure his wife's release.

The grandfather was summoned to the KGB.

When he refused to give money — because almost nothing remained — he was taken into another room.

The floor there was covered with dry peas.

They forced the grandfather to kneel and crawl across the room on all fours. When he stopped from pain, they kicked him and shouted:

"Go on! Go on! Until you give the money!"

To make it worse, they sat on his back like on a horse. And all the while they sang:

"Bring the money and go home."
"Bring the money and go home..."

When he lost consciousness, they splashed water on his face and began again — even louder.

Either you promise to bring money, or you lose consciousness. There were no other options.

He broke and promised.

They released him. He brought everything he had left and handed it over.

That was a mistake.

If he brought money once — that meant there must be more.

The abuse was repeated, even more brutally. His knees were already shattered from the first time.

"Bring even more money and go home..."

They tortured him to such a state that he lost consciousness and did not regain it.

Only then did they understand that there was no money left —

and they released him.

Gratitude

After that, the grandfather would say:

"I am a lucky man. I was fortunate they let me out alive."

"I feel no anger. Only gratitude toward those who tortured me. They could have killed me — but they let me go."

That was how the system worked. People were grateful for not being killed — for being merely tortured.

After Lithuania gained independence, memorial plaques appeared on the KGB building in Vilnius, bearing the names of those who entered and never returned. These lists cover an entire city block.

Grandmother Feiga spent almost a year in prison. She was released directly from the courtroom.

All of the grandfather's suffering was not in vain — he spent everything on it.

The freedom of a loved one cost more than any money.

It was fortunate that during the search they did not find the underground workshop in the cellar, nor the hidden valuables.

In life, there are moments when you are ready to give up everything for the love and freedom of someone who truly matters to you.

Survival is not the absence of death.
It is the presence of memory.

The system disappears.
But what it teaches remains for a long time.

* * *

PART III
"Some things are carried not because we must —
but because we cannot let them go."

64

PART III

GRANDMOTHER AND HER SUITCASE
On a Home That Cannot Be Bought

67

Sometimes happiness

is simply not being alone

Grandmother Feiga was released from prison after a year.

She was no longer the same woman. She had become stronger, quieter, more inward-looking. Something inside her seemed to have changed forever.

Almost immediately after her release, her husband died. He could not survive the fact that the woman he loved had been sent to prison. All that time, he felt guilty, as if he himself were the cause of her suffering.

Those were the years when people spoke more and more about Israel — about a new life, about the Holy Land. Jews were leaving, abandoning their homes, their friends, their habits.

The Man Who Wanted to Leave

Around that time, Grandmother met an intelligent, tall, handsome man. He was one of those people who were ready to do anything just to leave for the Holy Land — Israel. For him, it was the goal of his entire life.

He persuaded her to marry him so they could apply for emigration together. He already had a family — a wife, children, and grandchildren. But he divorced, insisting that he was doing it for love.

Grandmother believed him. She wanted to think that it was all for feeling, not for departure.

Of course, her relatives said otherwise: "He's just using her to leave."

But she did not want to listen.

Grandmother had a relative in Israel who was willing to take her in.

They married and soon submitted their documents for emigration to Israel. Everyone assured them that two pensioners would receive permission without difficulty.

But he did not believe it.

And indeed — a few months later, they received permission to leave.

Death from Happiness

He — *a healthy man who had never complained even about a cold — suddenly began to behave strangely. As if excitement had robbed him of peace: he fussed, bought unnecessary things.*

"We need to buy this, we need to take care of that," he repeated all day long.

They already had plane tickets: first to Moscow, and from there to Israel.

In the morning, they were supposed to go to the airport.

They agreed on the time when Boris's father would drive them.

All the suitcases were packed.

In the evening, they shared a farewell dinner — laughter, tears, suitcases by the door.

At night, when they lay down to sleep, his heart seized. He was taken straight from the house to the hospital.

There, without regaining consciousness, he died — on the very night when the plane was scheduled for the morning.

With tears in her eyes, Grandmother asked the doctor:

"What did he die of? He was never ill. His heart worked like a clock."

The doctor answered with a single sentence:

"You won't believe it... this man died of happiness."

He suffered a cerebral hemorrhage.

His heart could not withstand it — it pumped too much blood from the joy that tomorrow he was flying to Israel.

The Little Suitcase

After her husband's funeral, Grandmother packed a small suitcase — the same one that held her documents, a few dresses, and photographs — left everything behind: children, grandchildren, her home, and left alone.

She flew to Israel with her little suitcase.

In Israel, she was taken in by Aunt Ester, a wealthy, strict woman living in Tel Aviv. They began to live together.

Grandmother helped her around the house.

After some time, the Israeli government allocated her a small apartment of her own.

By the Sea

One day, Grandmother was walking with Aunt Ester along the main street that led straight to the sea. The sun burned her eyes; the air smelled of coffee and dust.

And suddenly Aunt Ester said:

"Why did you come here and burden me? You left your children, your grandchildren — and now what?"

Those words struck harder than anything before.

A woman had abandoned her entire life, her children, to come to Israel — and heard this.

At that moment, Grandmother thought she no longer needed anything in this life.

She wanted to walk straight to the sea without stopping, to enter the water and drown. Everything inside her was calling her there — where there would be silence.

That was all she wanted at that moment.

German Speech

But at the very edge of the sea, she suddenly heard German being spoken.

Two young men were laughing, talking loudly.

She stopped — the German language was native to her, reminding her of her youth.

She spoke German fluently — and in that moment, it was as if she returned to reality.

She approached them and quietly said in German:

"Excuse me, I don't know how to get home. I live in Ramat Gan — here is the address. Could you help me?"

"We're heading that way!" they replied. "Get in, we'll give you a ride."

They put her in the car and drove off.

Grandmother noticed that they were driving for a long time and that nothing outside the window looked familiar. She grew uneasy.

"Where are you taking me?" she asked nervously.

"Don't worry," they said. "We just need to stop somewhere briefly, then we'll go on."

"I only want to go home! You promised to take me home!"

The young men exchanged glances.

"Don't scare the grandmother," one said. "We'll take her home. We'll sort things out later."

And they really did take her straight to her house.

She jumped out of the car and ran away without looking back.

Manus Morgenstern

A few days later, someone knocked on the door.

Grandmother could not imagine who it might be. She looked through the peephole and saw a small elderly man.

"Who are you, and what do you want?" she asked through the door.

"Forgive me," he said in German. "Those were my nephews who gave you a ride. They wanted to take you to me first, then home, but you became frightened."

He asked permission to come in and talk.

Grandmother saw that he looked respectable and spoke with courtesy. She opened the door and let him in.

"What do you want?" she asked cautiously.

"I sincerely apologize for my nephews," he said. "They meant well."

"I would like to offer you a job. My wife recently passed away. She was a Polish Jew and cooked excellent European food.

I cannot eat in any restaurant. If you know how to cook, please come — at least once a day."

He offered Grandmother work — to cook European meals for him at least once a day.

That was how Manus Morgenstern entered her life. He turned out to be the owner of a chain of electronics stores in Germany.

He was a very wealthy man. When he retired, he bought a house in Israel and decided to spend his old age in the Holy Land, having left everything to his children.

Grandmother thought it over and agreed. Thus began her new life.

She came to his house every day and cooked lunches. She always cooked well — and everyone loved her food.

In time, Manus suggested that she live with him:

"Why walk back and forth every day? I have a large house. I'll pay you more. You'll cook breakfast, lunch, and dinner.

You'll have your own room."

Grandmother agreed.

She began helping Boris's family and sent money back to Lithuania.

"Don't Look"

*W*hen Boris came to Israel, he met his grandmother again.

They were walking along the main street of the city. The street was wide, noisy, flooded with light, with shop windows stretching along both sides.

Manus was walking ahead.

Grandmother and Boris were a little behind.

"Grandma, look," Boris said with delight. "What a huge television!"

"Yes, it's good," she replied calmly.

But she did not turn her head.

They walked on a little farther.

"Grandma, look at that beautiful bracelet," Boris said again, pointing at a shop window.

"Yes, it's beautiful," she answered just as calmly.

And again, she did not look.

Boris stopped.

"Grandma, I don't understand… Why don't you turn your head when I ask you to look at something?"

She stopped too and looked at him attentively.

"Do you want to see what happens if I look?"

"I do," Boris replied, surprised.

"Then watch."

She slowly turned her head toward the shop window.

Manus stopped.

He did not take another step.

Grandmother and Boris walked past him and stopped a few meters ahead.

Manus remained standing in place, motionless, as if someone were holding him back.

"Why isn't he going any farther?" Boris asked.

"Manus won't go anywhere," Grandmother said quietly, "until I come up to him and he knows what I looked at.

He has to buy it.

Only after that will we go on."

Manus was a grateful man. He loved her food, her voice, her presence.

For her sake, he was ready to give everything.

Manus owned a private harbor. In it stood a huge yacht.

In good weather, several times a year, they went out to sea.

The yacht had its own chef, captain, and waitstaff — full service.

They spent weeks at sea, thinking about nothing.

The Last Choice

Manus was around ninety years old. Grandmother took care of him. She helped him with everything — even bathing him in the shower.

One day she fell asleep. Manus did not want to wake her. He went to the bathroom by himself.

There, he slipped and fell. The hot water turned on, and he suffered severe burns.

When Grandmother Feiga woke up, he was still alive — just barely.

She called an ambulance, but it was already too late.

Manus died.

He bequeathed all his property to his children.

To Grandmother, he left only the large house in which they had lived together.

In his will, he wrote that Grandmother could live in that house for the rest of her life. No one had the right to touch her as long as she was alive.

But as a devoted admirer of the Holy Land, he wanted Grandmother to live and die precisely in Israel.

In addition, the children were obligated to transfer a large sum of money to her every month so that she could live comfortably.

But there was one condition:

All of this applied only as long as she lived in Israel.

If she left — everything would be canceled.

The payments would stop.

Return

*M*any years passed.

When Boris came from America to visit his grandmother, she opened a closet and said with tears in her eyes:

"Look... You won't find this much clothing in any store."

"Tell me — do I need all this?"

She gestured around the room.

"Look at this huge house. Workers come and clean. I don't need to do anything.

And I am living out my days alone... and I don't know what to do next."

Boris looked at her and said:

"Grandma, take that little suitcase. Remember the one you left us with when you went to Israel?

Leave all this behind.

Come to America. To us. To your family. We love you very much."

Grandmother began to cry. She embraced Boris tightly and said in a quiet, broken voice:

"Over the course of my life, I have lost many people who were dear to me.

And I understood one important thing.

Happiness cannot be bought — for any amount of money.

No wealth can replace the happiness you live within your family, in your home, in the place where you grew up."

Grandmother Feiga packed her little suitcase — small, old, faithful — left everything behind, and went to America.

There she lived out her final years surrounded by family.

Just as long ago, when they had all lived together in the Soviet Union.

Boris had already bought a house in Las Vegas. His father, mother, and sister came to join him.

He had been striving toward this all those years, from the moment he left home.

And at last, that time had come.

Sometimes happiness is simply not being alone.

People often fail to understand happiness while they are together.

*And only when they find themselves alone do they begin to realize
how important it was.*

*But unfortunately,
nothing can be changed,
and nothing can be brought back.*

* * *

Epilogue

What Remains

This book is not about the past.
The past always fades away.

It is about what a person carries with them
when there is nothing else left.

> *Things are lost.*
> *Money loses its value.*
> *Countries change their names.*
> *Systems collapse and are rebuilt.*

But there are things that do not yield to time.

> *Memory.*
> *Choice.*
> *And the ability to remain human.*

The fur coat saved a life — not because it was valuable,
but because, at the right moment,
someone chose to give warmth to another.

> *The underground workshop was not about money.*
> *It was about dignity and the attempt to preserve freedom*
> *where there was none.*

The small suitcase
turned out to be more important than palaces, yachts, and wealth,
because it contained a path back to family.

These stories are not about heroism.
They are about survival.

About decisions made quietly.
Without witnesses.
About love that needs no words.
About the price paid not for success,
but for the chance to remain oneself.

Sometimes it feels as if life is a chain of losses.

But looking back, you realize:
in truth, it is a process of selection.

Only what a person cannot live without remains.

Home.
Family.
Memory.

And if one day you must leave everything behind, perhaps you too will take with you
no more than a small suitcase.

89

If it holds love — that will be enough.

— Alex Avetis

90

Historical Note

This work is based on historical events and personal memories.

It reflects a time shaped by war, occupation, and political repression — particularly in Eastern Europe during the twentieth century. The narrative touches on life in Lithuania, including the city of Kaunas, the destruction of Jewish communities, the reality of ghettos, and the forced deportations to Siberia.

During the German occupation, Jewish populations were confined to ghettos — enclosed urban areas where people were isolated, deprived of basic resources, and subjected to violence, forced labor, and systematic persecution.

Later, under Soviet rule, many families were displaced or resettled into collective farms (kolkhozes), where life was defined by harsh labor, scarcity, and strict state control. Survival often depended not only on work, but on endurance and adaptability.

Everyday life during the Soviet period was closely monitored by state institutions. Among them were the KGB (Committee for State Security), responsible for political surveillance and repression, and the OBKhSS (Department for Combating the Theft of Socialist

Property), which investigated economic activity and unofficial trade.

In practice, these institutions often extended their power far beyond formal law. Small acts of private enterprise, possession of unregistered income, or even suspicion could lead to interrogation, confiscation of property, imprisonment, or exile. Fear became part of daily life, shaping not only actions, but also silence, caution, and the ways people related to one another.

While this narrative follows individual experiences, it is connected to broader historical realities that affected millions of people. The story reflects not only events, but also the moral choices individuals were forced to make within systems that allowed little room for freedom.

In the end, what remains is not the miracle we wait for, but the quiet choice that allows us to keep waiting.

Acknowledgements

This book was written to preserve memory — not only of events, but of the choices people make in difficult times.

The author expresses gratitude to those whose lives, stories, and silences made this work possible. Some of these stories were spoken aloud, others were carried quietly through generations, remaining in gestures, in pauses, and in what was left unsaid.

Special thanks are due to those who preserved these memories, often without knowing that one day they would become part of a larger story.

Among them is Hana, whose memory and voice carry this story across time.

— Alex Avetis

94

About the Author

Alex Avetis is a writer whose work explores memory, family history, and the quiet decisions that shape human lives. Drawing on personal and generational experience, he brings to life stories of survival, resilience, and the fragile thread that connects the past with the present.

*In **Grandmother and Her Suitcase**, he turns to an intimate family narrative — a story preserved through memory and passed down across time. Through this lens, his writing reflects not only historical reality, but the inner lives of those who lived through it.*

His work moves between documentary precision and literary reflection, focusing not on events themselves, but on the people within them — their choices, fears, and dignity.

He writes to preserve the moment when a person makes a choice — and becomes who they are.

— Alex Avetis